Mark and Michelle in the forest

MARCEL MARLIER

Mark and Michelle lived near a forest where hundreds of birds and animals had their homes.

One day they found a baby bird that had fallen out of its nest.

"Poor thing, he's a fledgling," said Mark. "That means he's only just learning to fly. Let's see if we can get him to take some food — he's so frightened and weak."

When the baby bird had eaten
a little of the food, Mark
laid him gently in some long grass
under the tree. He fluttered and
cheeped feebly at the children.
"Perhaps we should take him home
with us," said Michelle.
"No, it will be better just to leave
him quietly by himself. When he's
feeling stronger he will find his own
way back to the nest, or his mother
will come to help him."

So they left him there and went for a
long walk in the forest. Birds were
singing everywhere: the robin, the
thrush, the blackbird, and above them
all the lovely song of the lark.
A hare stood quite still with his
ears pricked up as the children ran
by hand in hand.

Further on in the forest a
family of red squirrels were
scampering along a branch.
The children crouched behind
a mossy tree stump to watch
them. The father squirrel
stared inquisitively at them,
his whiskers and tail quivering.

Michelle was so happy, she threw herself down on the soft ground.

"Shh... be quiet," said Mark. The squirrel scampered away up the tree. "You have to move very gently in the forest, and not say much, or you'll frighten all the creatures away and we won't be able to watch them."

His sister rolled over and lay on her back. She could smell the sweet scent of the woodland flowers near her face. The long grass tickled her neck. Looking up through the branches of the tree, she could see a mother bird feeding her young. She called softly to Mark to come and look.

Mark loved the woodland creatures and knew quite a lot about their ways. He lay down quietly beside his sister to watch.

The babies had their beaks wide open and were cheeping impatiently telling their mother to bring the insects she had been catching for them.

They looked funny, and not very pretty, with their spiky feathers and gaping mouths.

High up in the branches there were other nests too. Some were tiny and made of moss, and others were made of twigs or pieces of grass and straw. A pair of bullfinches stood proudly guarding their nest in a holly tree, and further off was a nightingale. "You should hear him singing at night," said Mark. "It is a beautiful song, and he goes on and on, while the other birds are silent."

Ratatatat... Ratatatat... A sharp tapping noise echoed
clearly through the forest. "It's a woodpecker,"
said Mark.
"He's striking the tree trunk with his sharp beak. He'll
be looking for grubs and insects under the bark."
In the soft wood of a dead tree they could see where
the woodpecker had dug a hole nearly a metre deep,
using his head like a chisel.

Mark bent down suddenly to look at something he had spotted on the soft earth.

"It's an empty wren's nest," he said.

"See how they weave their nests like a small ball, leaving a tiny hole for going in and out.

I wonder how this one got here?

What can have happened to the birds?"

The children soon found the answer.
Lying in and around the nest were some
scattered feathers and broken pieces of shell.
"It looks as if an animal has frightened away
the parent birds and eaten the eggs," said
Mark.
"There are many creatures in the forest who
steal birds' eggs for their food. Some prowl
at night, and others hunt stealthily in the
daytime."
The children crept silently forward, pretending
to be wild animals stalking their prey.
"It seems very cruel," said Michelle sadly.
"But I suppose every creature must find food
to eat.
I wonder which animal stole these eggs?
Perhaps if we keep very quiet
we shall see him."

"I shouldn't think so," said Mark.
"He will be well hidden by now.
But I think the thief may
have had green eyes,
sharp teeth, whiskers and
a bushy tail with six black
rings around it. Can you
guess?"
"You mean a wild cat,"
whispered his sister.

They came to a clearing in the forest where a pair of young roe deer were lying in the shade of a tree.

"Don't touch them, Michelle," warned Mark as she stretched out her hand to stroke the tiny animals. "If their mother smells your scent on them she won't come near them again. She must be grazing a little way off.

See how the white spots on their fur look like dappled sunlight falling through the leaves?

It helps the babies to remain hidden among the trees and bushes."

Mark said thoughtfully, "If we
come back here one day in the
autumn, early in the morning when
it is still misty and the leaves are just turning red and brown, we
might see the full-grown stags charging each other, clashing
their antlers together so that the whole forest rings with the
noise."

"Later on in the year, when the frost is
crisp on the ground and winter snows
sprinkle the trees like icing sugar, the deer
leave their secret places in the heart of the forest
to look for food.
Sometimes they come to the very edge
of the woodland. And then you might
see families of wild boar, too,
digging in the frozen ground
for roots and acorns."

"Are there wild boar in the forest?" exclaimed Michelle.
"Do you think we might see one?"
A large horned owl stared solemnly after the
children with his yellow, unblinking eyes. The
sun was sinking now behind the trees,
slanting its shafts of light between the
trunks.

One by one the night-time creatures
were beginning to appear. And suddenly
snuffling along the ground, came a large
boar. Michelle could see his tusks clearly.
A little way off was the female with her
striped young ones.

Further on four little fox cubs peered cautiously at the children from the safety of their lair.

"How sweet they look," said Michelle. "They may seem sweet now," said Mark, "but they are considered the most cunning of woodland animals.

I expect that their mother, the vixen, has gone off now to hunt and steal for their supper. She may even be robbing a farmer's hen-house at this moment!"

"And think
what tricks
a fox will play on
other animals," Mark
went on.
"He will watch a
badger making himself
a new burrow, building
it very carefully with
passages leading to
different rooms, and making
it warm and cosy.
Then when it is finished he
goes out to hunt for food,
and before you know where
you are, the fox has slipped
in through the door and set
up house there himself!"
"Look! Isn't that a badger
along there?" whispered
Michelle.
"Yes. He's out for a walk
in the evening air along
the bank of the stream."

"It's getting quite dark,"
said Michelle. "We'd better go home."
The forest was now full of strange noises —
the scurrying of little creatures, rats and voles

and mice among the fallen leaves. The flapping of
a kestrel's wings swooping up to a branch with his prey. The
plaintive call of the tawny owl echoing through the treetops...
tuwhoo... tuwhoo... whoo...

"We've had a lovely day," said Michelle. "But I didn't know the forest was full of so many savage creatures."

"Oh yes," said her brother. "Many animals must hunt to live. The pine marten takes eggs and young birds... and sometimes he'll even go after a squirrel."